To Ryan and Phoenix, the loves of my life who inspire me every day. Never stop dreaming! Mommy loves you to the moon and back and more than all of the stars in the sky.

www.mascotbooks.com

The Truth Fairy

Second Printing. This Mascot Books edition printed in 2022.

For more information, please contact:
Mascot Books
620 Herndon Parkway, Suite 320
Herndon, VA 20170
info@mascotbooks.com

Library of Congress Control Number: 2021910923

CPSIA Code: PRT0122B
ISBN-13: 978-1-64307-393-4

Printed in the United States

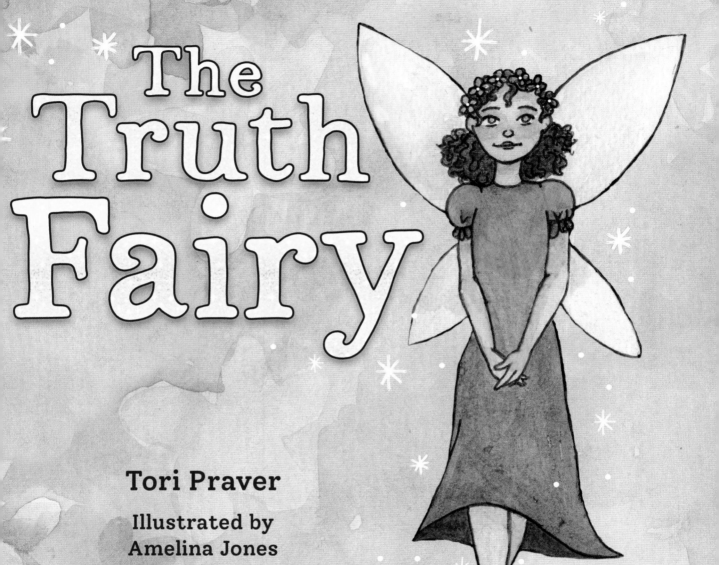

The Truth Fairy

Tori Praver

Illustrated by
Amelina Jones

Once upon a time, there lived a little girl named Lily. She was a very kind and smart little girl. But Lily had one small problem. She liked to tell fibs.

Do you know what a fib is? A fib is a story that isn't true. Lily told fibs because they let her get away with things. She would fib about cleaning up, brushing her teeth, and playing with her slime in places she was not supposed to.

She would even tell fibs about eating candy or treats when she wasn't supposed to. Sometimes, fibs can get you into trouble, and sometimes, they can even hurt other people. So, it is very important to always tell the truth.

One night before bed, Lily's mama asked if she had brushed her teeth. Lily knew she hadn't brushed her teeth yet, but instead of telling the truth, Lily told a fib.

That same night, Lily's mama decided to tell her about the Truth Fairy. She explained to Lily that every night before she went to sleep, a beautiful, yet very tiny lady called the Truth Fairy came to Lily's mama and told her the truth about all the things that had happened that day.

The Truth Fairy almost always told happy stories, but sometimes she had to tell the truth about a fib or a lie that had been told.

Lily was in shock to hear about this fairy and knew that she could never, ever tell a fib again. She woke up the very next morning and asked her mama if the Truth Fairy had come.

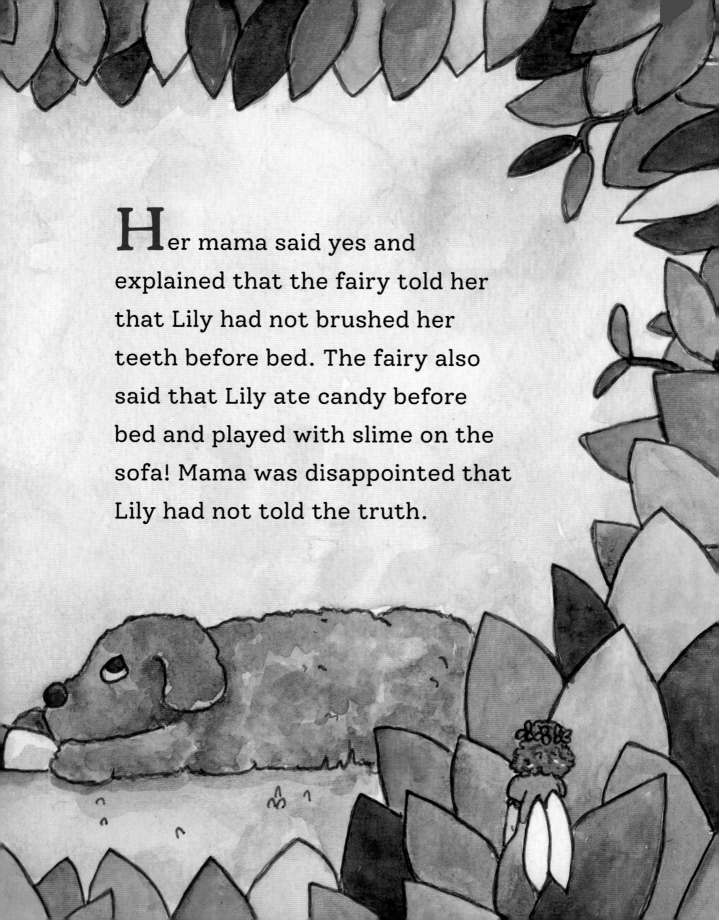

Her mama said yes and explained that the fairy told her that Lily had not brushed her teeth before bed. The fairy also said that Lily ate candy before bed and played with slime on the sofa! Mama was disappointed that Lily had not told the truth.

Lily felt really guilty about fibbing and promised herself and her mama that she would always tell the truth from that day forward.

The next night, when Lily was playing before bed, Mama asked if she had brushed her teeth yet. Lily wanted to keep playing, but she knew now that the Truth Fairy was watching!

"No, Mama," she said. "But I'll brush them now!"

The
End

About the Author

Tori Praver grew up on the beaches of Maui before spending years in New York City and then settling in Los Angeles to raise her children, Ryan and Phoenix. While enjoying her busy life with her kids, she realized she had a knack for telling great stories to her children. This inspired her to create *The Truth Fairy*. She now resides in Los Angeles with her husband, two children, and their dog, Maui.